WELL I NEVER!

WELL I NEVER!

Text by
Heather Eyles

Pictures by
Tony Ross

Andersen Press • London

Text copyright © 1988 by Heather Eyles
Illustrations copyright © 1988 by Tony Ross
The rights of Heather Eyles and Tony Ross to be identified as the author and illustrator of this work have
been asserted by them in accordance with the Copyright, Designs and Patents Act, 1988.
First published in Great Britain in 1988 by Andersen Press Ltd., 20 Vauxhall Bridge Road,
London SW1V 2SA.
This paperback edition first published in 1997 by Andersen Press Ltd.
Published in Australia by Random House Australia Pty., 20 Alfred Street, Milsons Point,
Sydney, NSW 2061. All rights reserved. Colour separated in Switzerland by Photolitho AG,
Offsetreproduktionen, Gossau, Zürich. Printed and bound in Italy by Grafiche AZ, Verona.

10   9   8   7   6   5   4   3   2   1

British Library Cataloguing in Publication Data available.

ISBN 0 86264 787 8

This book has been printed on acid-free paper

It was Monday morning. Time to go to school, and Polly wasn't dressed. As usual.

"Go and get your tee-shirt," said Mum.
"It's in the bedroom."

"I can't go in there," said Polly. "There's
a witch in there."
"Nonsense!" said Mum.

"And your shorts are in the bathroom," said Mum.

"Oh, I can't go in there," said Polly.
"There's a vampire in there."
"Rubbish!" said Mum.

"By the way," said Mum, "your socks are on the stairs."

"Nope, I can't go up there," said Polly.
"There's a werewolf up there."
"Fiddlesticks!" said Mum.

"Don't forget, your shoes are in the cupboard under the stairs," said Mum.

"No, I'm not going in there," said Polly.
"There's a ghost in there."
"Balderdash!" said Mum.

So Mum went to get the
clothes herself.
"Toads and slugs'
bottoms!" shrieked the
witch, who looked very
fetching in Polly's tee-
shirt.

"What a lovely neck you have, m'dear!" murmured the vampire, who was just trying on Polly's shorts.

"Grrr!" growled the
werewolf, who was
having a lovely slobbery
chew of Polly's socks.

The ghost said nothing.
Not anything at all. But
she did a spooky dance in
Polly's shoes.

Mum ran all the way back to the kitchen.
"Well I never!" she said.

"You're joking, aren't you, Mum?" said
Polly.
"Am I?" answered Mum.
"There aren't really any monsters out
there, are there?" said Polly.
"Aren't there?" answered Mum.

So they went out to look together, hand in hand, down the passage,

up the stairs,

past the bathroom,

and into the bedroom.

"Phew!" said Mum.

"Told you!" said Polly. "And now I think
I'll get dressed if you don't mind."